AF531212

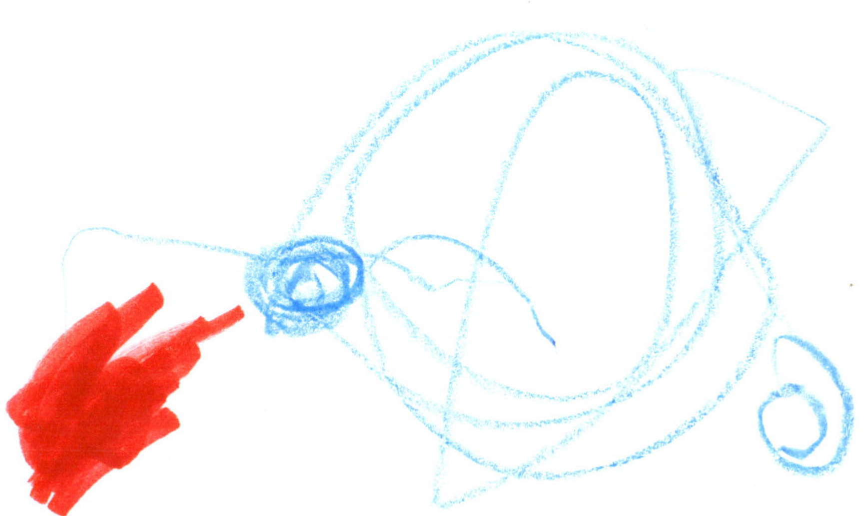

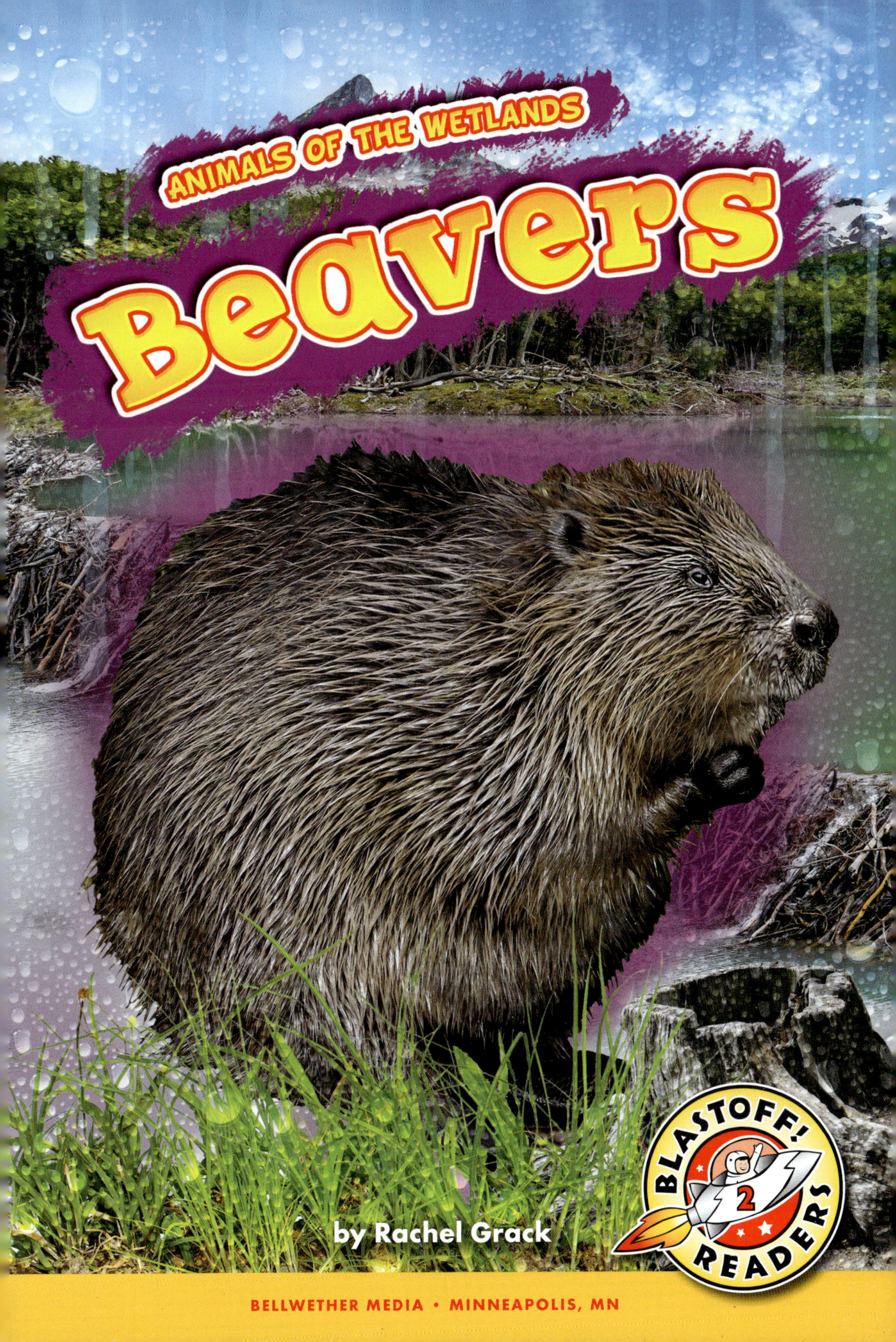

ANIMALS OF THE WETLANDS
Beavers
by Rachel Grack
BLASTOFF! READERS
2
BELLWETHER MEDIA • MINNEAPOLIS, MN

Note to Librarians, Teachers, and Parents:

Blastoff! Readers are carefully developed by literacy experts and combine standards-based content with developmentally appropriate text.

Level 1 provides the most support through repetition of high-frequency words, light text, predictable sentence patterns, and strong visual support.

Level 2 offers early readers a bit more challenge through varied simple sentences, increased text load, and less repetition of high-frequency words.

Level 3 advances early-fluent readers toward fluency through increased text and concept load, less reliance on visuals, longer sentences, and more literary language.

Level 4 builds reading stamina by providing more text per page, increased use of punctuation, greater variation in sentence patterns, and increasingly challenging vocabulary.

Level 5 encourages children to move from "learning to read" to "reading to learn" by providing even more text, varied writing styles, and less familiar topics.

Whichever book is right for your reader, Blastoff! Readers are the perfect books to build confidence and encourage a love of reading that will last a lifetime!

This edition first published in 2020 by Bellwether Media, Inc.

Library of Congress Cataloging-in-Publication Data

Names: Koestler-Grack, Rachel A., 1973- author.
Title: Beavers / by Rachel Grack.
Description: Minneapolis, MN : Bellwether Media, Inc., 2020. | Series: Blastoff! Readers. Animals of the Wetlands | Audience: Age 5-8. | Audience: K to Grade 3. | Includes bibliographical references and index.
Identifiers: LCCN 2018051140 (print) | LCCN 2018051553 (ebook) | ISBN 9781618915269 (ebook) | ISBN 9781626179868 (hardcover : alk. paper)
Subjects: LCSH: Beavers--Juvenile literature. | Wetland animals--Juvenile literature.
Classification: LCC QL737.R632 (ebook) | LCC QL737.R632 K64 2020 (print) | DDC 599.7--dc23
LC record available at https://lccn.loc.gov/2018051140

Editor: Betsy Rathburn Designer: Josh Brink

Printed in the United States of America, North Mankato, MN.

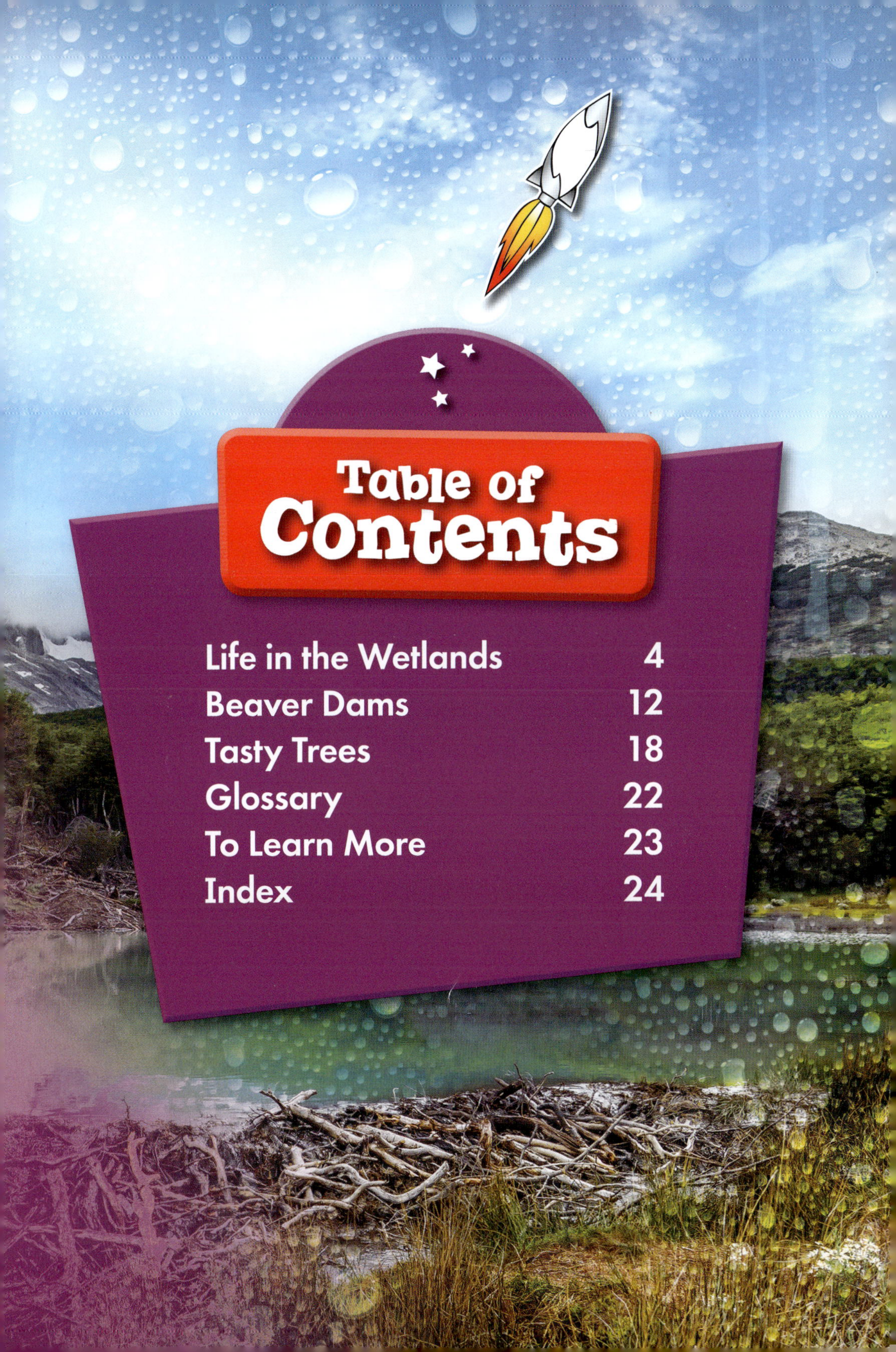

Table of Contents

Life in the Wetlands

Beavers are busy wetland **rodents**. They live near lakes, rivers, and streams.

These critters are found across North America, Europe, and Asia. They love their watery **biome**!

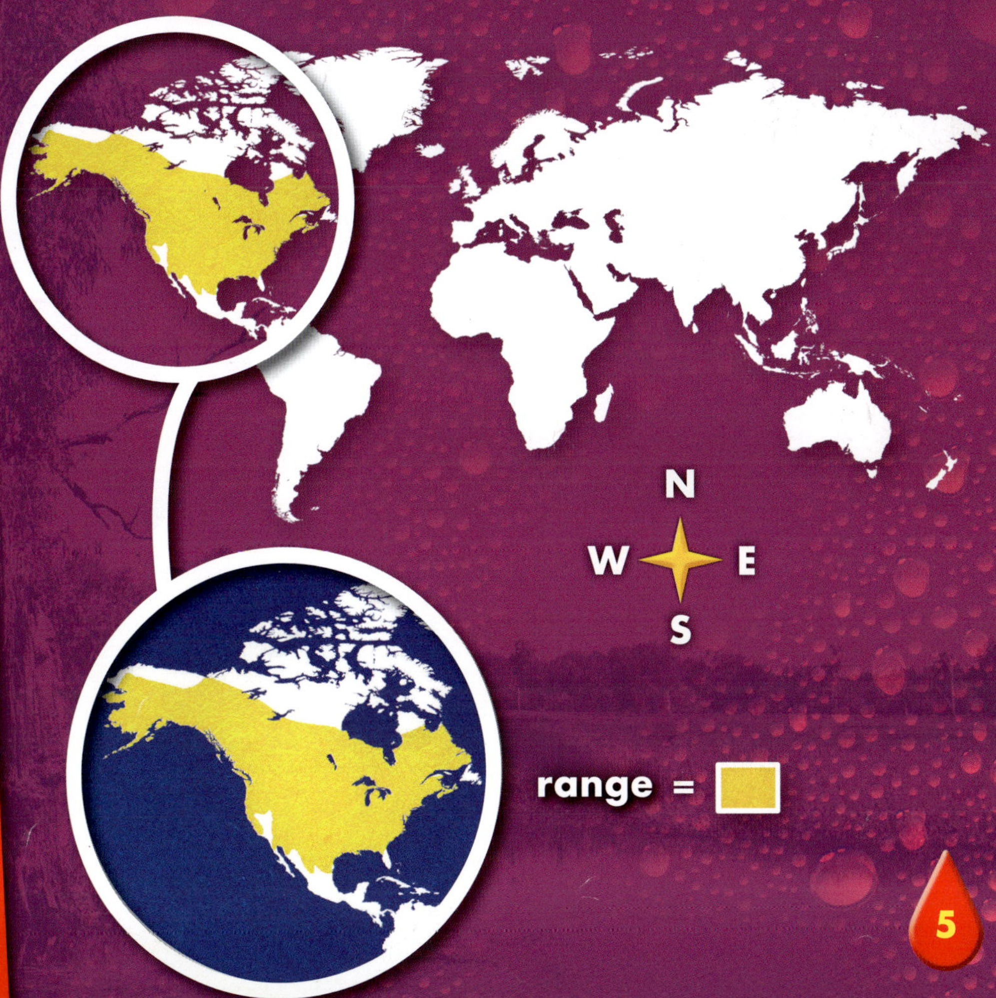

Beavers have **adapted** to spend time in water. Clear inner eyelids help them see underwater.

Their ears and **nostrils** close to keep water out.

Beaver lips close behind their teeth. They can carry and **gnaw** branches underwater.

Webbed back feet make beavers great swimmers. Paddle-shaped tails steer them along.

Special Adaptations

Beavers stay warm and dry in wetland waters. They have thick **undercoats** and extra fat for warmth.

Their oily fur is **waterproof**!

Beaver Dams

dam

Beavers help shape the wetlands they live in. They build **dams** to block streams.

Valleys, fields, and forests become flooded. A beaver **colony** can move in!

The wetlands hold many **predators**. Beavers build **lodges** to stay safe and warm.

When danger is near, beavers dive!
They swim to their underwater doorways.
Predators stay out!

American Beaver Stats

Least Concern	Near Threatened	Vulnerable	Endangered	Critically Endangered	Extinct in the Wild	Extinct

conservation status: least concern

life span: up to 24 years

Beavers use **scent glands** to mark their homes. This helps keep other beavers away.

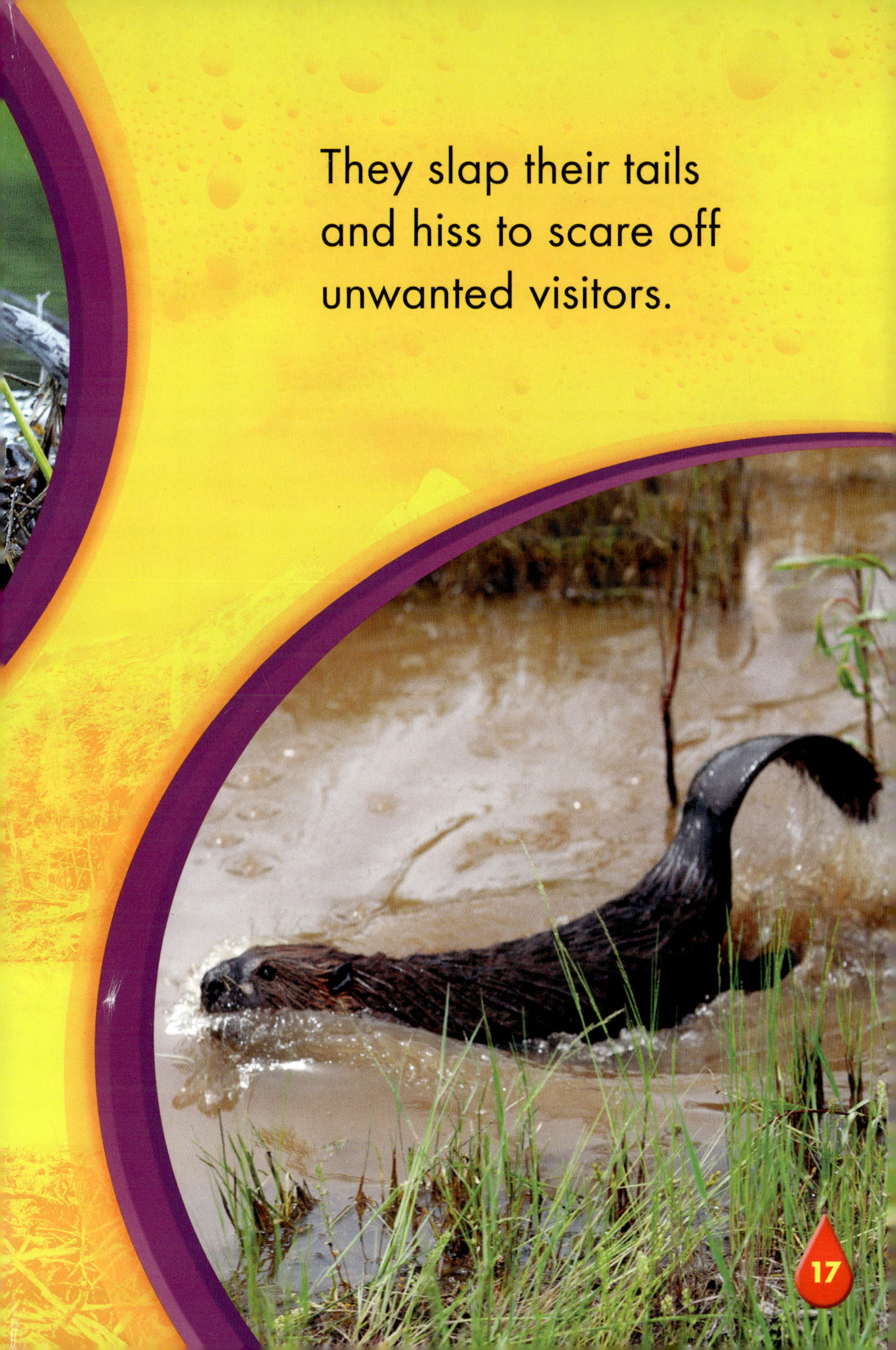

They slap their tails and hiss to scare off unwanted visitors.

Tasty Trees

Beavers have long front teeth. Iron makes their teeth strong. It also turns their teeth orange.

These critters chew through tough bark. They dig out tasty **cambium**.

Beaver teeth never stop growing. The backs of their teeth wear away faster than the fronts.

This keeps their teeth sharp. Beavers have a lot of chewing to do!

Glossary

adapted—changed over a long period of time

biome—a large area with certain plants, animals, and weather

cambium—the soft, thin layer beneath tree bark from which beavers get food

colony—a group of one or more families of beavers

dams—structures made by beavers from branches, twigs, and mud that block water

gnaw—to chew

lodges—beaver homes built out of branches, twigs, and mud

nostrils—the two openings of the nose

predators—animals that hunt other animals for food

rodents—animals that gnaw on their food

scent glands—body parts that spray odor

undercoats—layers of short, soft hair or fur that keep some animals warm

waterproof—able to keep water from soaking through

webbed—having an area of skin between the fingers or toes

To Learn More

AT THE LIBRARY

Donohue, Moira Rose. *Beavers.* New York, N.Y.: Children's Press, 2019.

Reingold, Adam. *The Beaver's Lodge: Building With Leftovers.* New York, N.Y.: Bearport Publishing, 2019.

Wilson, Emily. *Inside Beaver Lodges.* New York, N.Y.: PowerKids Press, 2016.

ON THE WEB

FACTSURFER

Factsurfer.com gives you a safe, fun way to find more information.

1. Go to www.factsurfer.com.
2. Enter "beavers" into the search box and click 🔍.
3. Select your book cover to see a list of related web sites.

Index

The images in this book are reproduced through the courtesy of: O Brasil que poucos conhecem, front cover (background); Sergei Brik, front cover (beaver); Frank Fichtmueller, p. 4; Nature Picture Library/ Alamy, p. 6; Sylvie Bouchard, p. 7; Jaime Espinosa, p. 8; Musat, p. 9; Christian Musat, p. 9 (top); NancyS, p. 10; All Canada Photos/ Alamy, p. 11; Ronnie Howard, p. 12; Robert McGouey/ SuperStock, p. 13; Charlie Hamilton James/ Getty Images, p. 14; Enrique Aguirre, p. 15; Chase Dekker, p. 16; Stan Tekiela/ Getty Images, p. 17; Kerry Hargrove, p. 18; RUBENBON10, p. 19 (top left); seeyou, p. 19 (top right); Cjwhitewine, p. 19 (bottom); Mauritius/ SuperStock, p. 20; Jeff Foott/ SuperStock, p. 21; Zadiraka Evgenii, p. 23.

LOVE IN "THE CITY DIFFERENT"

Bask in the muted tones of desert pink and mauve that complement the elegant white suit worn by the ever-desirable Bradley Roberson III. Newly arrived in Santa Fe, he has come West to realize an affair with local luminary John Aaron. Here in "the city different"—where opera, art, and adobe are regarded with equal passion and zeal—Bradley is acquiring a reputation as a mischievously manipulative young man and a breaker of hearts. And John Aaron is indulging in a sulk of major proportion.

A stylish novel about a feisty romantic tug-of-war, DESERT FABULOSO is also about sons and fathers—Bradley's, who was also gay, and John's, who most definitely was not—and about two very contemporary men struggling to come to terms with their pasts. But surrounding these savory stories is always the city of Santa Fe itself, full of complexity and contradiction with its several cultures—Anglo, Indian, Spanish, very ancient, very modern.

LISA LOVENHEIM, a graduate of Vassar College, lived for several years in Santa Fe, where she was involved in the art world. A former editor at Northland Press in Flagstaff, Arizona, she also worked in bilingual education on the Navajo Reservation. DESERT FABULOSO is her first novel.